I HAVE TWO DADDIES
(An Earthly Daddy and A Heavenly Daddy)

Written by Lynn Calvin Plater
Illustrated by Maria Rask

AuthorHouse™
1663 Liberty Drive
Bloomington, IN 47403
www.authorhouse.com
Phone: 833-262-8899

Because of the dynamic nature of the Internet, any web addresses or links contained in this book may have changed
since publication and may no longer be valid. The views expressed in this work are solely those of the author and do
not necessarily reflect the views of the publisher, and the publisher hereby disclaims any responsibility for them.

Any people depicted in stock imagery provided by Getty Images are models,
and such images are being used for illustrative purposes only.
Certain stock imagery © Getty Images.

This book is printed on acid-free paper.

ISBN: 978-1-4343-6943-7 (sc)
ISBN: 978-1-4817-1227-9 (e)

Print information available on the last page.

Published by AuthorHouse 03/10/2022

authorHOUSE®

Dedication
1950-1997

This book is dedicated to my father, Charles Calvin, Jr. Thank you, Daddy, for your love, inspiration, strength, laughter, encouragement, advice, listening ear, and helping me become the woman I am today.

I have two daddies. One I can see and one I can't see. Both of my daddies love me.

Let me tell you about my daddies.

The daddy I can see lives on Earth with me.
This daddy only has one name. His name is
Charles.

The daddy I can see loves me, and he takes care of me like the Daddy I can't see told him to take care of me.

How do I know the daddy I can see loves me? That's easy, because he goes to work so he can buy me clothes and food.

He bought a house so I can have a room to call my own.

My Room

He bought a bed for me to lay my head down. He bought toys for me to play with and books for me to read.

He takes me out to have fun, and listens when I want to talk.

At night before I go to bed, he tells me about the Daddy I can't see.

The Daddy I can't see lives in Heaven. He has many names, but most people call Him "God."

How do I know that the Daddy I can't see loves me? That's easy, because He gave me a daddy I can touch and see, and he takes care of me.

The biggest reason that I know He loves me is because He made a way for me to live with Him forever ...

By giving me a Big Brother (Jesus) who I can't see, but who got in BIG TROUBLE (dying for sin) for me on a BIG TREE (the cross). John 3:16

If I want to live with the Daddy I can't see who loves me, all I have to do is tell Him that I am sorry for the trouble (sin), ask Him to forgive me, and believe that my Big Brother took my place.

And one day, you won't see me, because I will be with the Daddy I can't see—FOREVER (EVERLASTING LIFE). Romans 10:9-10

I HAVE TWO DADDIES

AND THEY BOTH LOVE ME!!!

Scriptural Reference

For God so loved the world that He gave His only begotten Son, that whoever believes in Him should not perish but have eternal life.
John 3:16 (KJV)

Scriptural Reference

That if you confess with your mouth the Lord Jesus and believe in your heart that God raised Him from the dead, you will be saved. For with the heart one believes unto righteousness, and with the mouth confession is made unto salvation. Romans 10:9-10 (KJV)

The Invitation for a Daddy that you can't see who loves you.

If you want a Daddy who loves you but you can't see, I'll share my Daddy with you; please pray with me.

Prayer for a Daddy that you can't see who loves you.

Dear God,

    I have learned and believe that You sent Your Son, Jesus, to die on the cross for me. I also believe that you raised Him from the dead so I can live with You forever. I am sorry for the sin. Please forgive me. Thank You for Your Son Jesus.

    Thank You, Jesus, for dying on the cross for me. Jesus, please come into my heart so I can have You and a Daddy I can't see who loves me and I can live with forever.

In Jesus Name,
Amen

HALLELUJAH! Today, YOU have a Daddy and Big Brother who you can't see but who love you so much, and one day, you will live with them forever.

Please complete your
Praise Certificate

PRAISE CERTIFICATE

Praise God, Today_____

date

I,_____,
have a Daddy and Big Brother I
can't see but loves me so much and
one day, I will live with them
forever!

Some Names of God

Jehovah- God

Jehovah Jireh- God who provides

Jehovah Shaloam- God of Peace

Jehovah Rapha- God who heals

Jehovah Raah- God who is my shepherd

Pronunciation of Names of God

G ho va

G ho va ji ra

G ho va sha lome

G ho va raf fa

G ho va ra a

Match the Names

Jehovah	Shepherd
Jehovah Jireh	Peace
Jehovah Shaloam	Healer
Jehovah Rapha	Provider
Jehovah Raah	God

Draw a picture of yourself with your Daddy and Big Brother who you can't see but who love you very much.

Note to Parents

Dear Parents,

If your child was sincere about accepting the Invitation to a Daddy they can't see but loves them, PLEASE ENCOURAGE their spiritual growth by praying for them, reading the Bible together, taking them to Sunday school and church.

Humbly submitted,

Lynn Calvin

Lynn Calvin

Author

ACKNOWLEDGMENTS

Thank you to the Daddy I can't see (God) for giving me the book to write.

Thank you to my Big Brother (Jesus) for strengthening me to be obedient in writing this book.

Thank you to the Holy Spirit for encouraging me to see the vision, write the vision, and see the vision come to pass.

Thank you to my grandfather, Charles Savage, who financially assisted and encouraged me to publish the vision.

Thank you to my pastor, Rev. Dr. Douglas E. Summers, for reviewing and theologically editing the book.

Thank you principals, Lilly McElveen and Margarett Shipley, and former principals Elizabeth Craig and Dr. Maxine Wood and Rev. Richard T. Adams, Auntie Deacon (Helen Davis) and Deacon Frank Chase for reviewing the book for age-appropriateness and grammatical errors. Thank you Visionettes Liturgical Dance Ministry, who I believe God used to inspire me to write this book. Thank you to everyone else whose name I did not mention, for all of your prayers, support, and encouragement.

About the Author

Lynn resides in Baltimore, Maryland. She has three grown daughters, Monique, Khristina and D'Anita and four granddaughters, Taylor, Cierra, Shantae and Shawna. She attended Coppin State University, formerly Coppin State College, where she received her Bachelor of Science degree in Biology. Currently, she is working as a Sr. Research Programs Supervisor at Johns Hopkins University located in Baltimore, Maryland.

As an active member of Providence Baptist Church, she is the coordinator of the Visionettes Liturgical Dance Ministry (children and youth between the ages of 3-18) and the Ministry of Dance (adults between the ages of 19-50). In addition, she is a Girl Scout Leader, a member of Bible Study for Today's Living Sunday School class, the Board of Christian Education, and the Psalmodists of Praise Choir. She is also a member of Restoration Dance Ministry which is a community based liturgical dance ministry and a partner with the International Liturgical Dance Fellowship located in Baltimore.

Lynn loves the Lord and loves to teach children about the Lord.

About the Illustrator

Maria Rask graduated Black Hills State University in 1999 with a Bachelors of Art. Her dream was to illustrate children's books. August of 2007, Maria and her family were victims of a natural disaster that flooded the town they had just moved to the day before.

They lost everything and were rendered homeless for over three months. Because of the flood, Maria's husband Clayton no longer had a job. Maria was no longer able to work as her art supplies and equipment had been destroyed.

It all seemed hopeless, but there is a purpose to everything that happens. Maria's husband was offered a wonderful job in his home town. Maria was able to replace her equipment and get enough work to replenish her destroyed portfolios.

Maria had faith and never gave up on her dreams. Utilizing her knowledge, skills and wild imagination, she currently illustrates children's books from home while running after her three year old son Kael with the help of her eight year old daughter Laura.

Printed in the United States
by Baker & Taylor Publisher Services